MARGARINE AND MARBLES

NICOLA MOON * MARK OLIVER

Go Bananas

Crabtree Publishing Company

www.crabtreebooks.com

PMB 16A, 350 Fifth Avenue,
Suite 3308,
New York, NY 10118

616 Welland Avenue,
St. Catharines, Ontario
Canada, L2M 5V6

To Megan,
who can move mountains
N.M.

For Lorcan and Lara
M.O.

Cataloging-in-Publication data is available at the Library of Congress.

Published by Crabtree Publishing in 2006
First published in 2005 by Egmont Books Ltd.
Text copyright © Nicola Moon 2005
Illustrations copyright © Mark Oliver 2005
The Author and Illustrator have asserted their moral rights.
Paperback ISBN 0-7787-2698-3
Reinforced Hardcover Binding ISBN 0-7787-2676-2

1 2 3 4 5 6 7 8 9 0 Printed in Italy 4 3 2 1 0 9 8 7 6 5

Contents

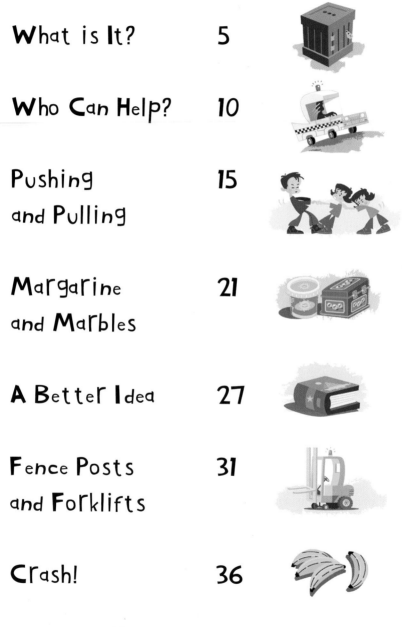

Go Bananas

WHAT IS IT?

One morning there was a loud banging on the door. Tom went to open it. It was Mrs. Ramsbottom from down the street. She looked very angry.

"Is it yours?" she asked. "I'm late for work, and I can't get my car out."

Tom looked outside.

I want
it moved!

He saw an enormous wooden crate. It was taller than his dad and wider than a car. It had three small holes along the top and a door with a padlock at one end. It was blocking half the street and it was making Mrs. Ramsbottom very upset.

"It's not mine," said Tom. "What is it?"

"It's an obstruction, that's what it is," said Mrs. Ramsbottom.

Tom's mom and his little brother Pip came to see what all the fuss was about.

"It wasn't there last night," said Tom's mom.

"Well, it's there now and I want it moved," huffed Mrs. Ramsbottom.

Hmm.

I wonder what it is?

Mrs. Ramsbottom wasn't the only one who had noticed the crate.

Zoe and Chloe, the twins, were halfway up a street light. They were trying to peer through the holes at the top of the crate.

Sanjeev was passing on his bicycle.

It's too dark in there.

"I think it's full of gold!" he said.

"Or jewels!" said Tom.

"It could be full of chocolate!" said Chloe.

"Oh, yum!" said Zoe.

"I think there's a monster inside!" said Pip, who was only three.

"Don't be silly," said Tom.

"Whatever it is, it's in my way," said Mrs. Ramsbottom, and she stormed off to call a taxi.

Tom's dad called the police.

WHO CAN HELP?

A few minutes later a police car raced up the street with its lights flashing.

It stopped beside the crate.

"Well hello!"

"Who's crate is this?" asked the officer.

"We don't know," said Tom. "It was here when we got up."

"It doesn't look dangerous," said the officer. "But I'll cordon it off just in case."

He got a big roll of tape out of the car.

"Aren't you going to move it?" asked Tom's mom.

"Sorry," said the officer. "It's too big. Why don't you call the fire station?"

Tom's dad phoned the fire station, but as the crate wasn't on fire they couldn't help.

"Why don't you call the city?" suggested the lady on the phone. "They should move it."

Tom's dad phoned city hall. They said they would send someone out next Tuesday.

"Why don't you try calling the police," suggested the man on the phone.

"This is ridiculous!" said Tom's dad.

"Somebody must be able to do something."

Somebody was doing something. A meter reader was writing out a parking ticket. "Whatever it is, it can't park here," she said.

"Why don't we move it ourselves?" suggested Tom.

"It's too big," said Tom's mom.

"Where would we move it to?" asked Tom's dad.

"We could move it into the rest area at the end of the street," said Tom.

"That's uphill," said Zoe. "It's hard to move things uphill."

I can see for miles!

Tut, Tut!

What are we going to do?

"We could move it downhill to a parking lot," said Chloe.

"We'll need lots of people to help," said Tom's dad. "It looks very heavy."

"That's easy," said Zoe and Chloe, and they ran off down the street to find help.

Leave it to us!

PUSHING
AND PULLING

Before long, Zoe and Chloe
were back.

It seemed as though the whole
street had come to help.

John the letter carrier, Joe from
the café, Bill and Brenda
from the garage, Polly from the
corner store, Sanjeev with his
brother, Mrs. Evans from
number ten, old Mr. Brown
who was ninety-five, and
several people they'd never
seen before.

"Are you all ready?" Tom's dad asked. "One, two, three, PUSH!"

Everyone pushed as hard as they could.

They pushed until sweat poured down their faces and their arms ached.

But the crate didn't move.

Oof!

Nnng!

Phew!

Tom's mom handed
out lemonade and cookies.

"I think pulling would be better than
pushing," suggested Sanjeev, when
everyone had recovered.

Bill went to get some rope from
the garage. He tied it
firmly around
the crate.

"It's like a tug-of-war!" said Zoe, as everyone grabbed hold of the rope.

"Ready, everyone?" asked Bill. "One, two, three, PULL!"

Everyone pulled as hard as they could.

They pulled until their faces were red and their hands were burning.

But still the crate didn't move.

Biggest parcel I've ever seen.

"What on earth is in this crate?" asked Joe.

"I think it's full of rocks!" said Polly.

"Whatever it's full of, it's just too heavy," said Tom's mom, handing around more drinks.

"There must be a better way of moving it," said Tom. "It can't stay here forever."

"It would be easier to move it if the road was icy," said Sanjeev. "Ice makes things slippery."

"Like the time you slid all the way down the street on your bottom!" Chloe giggled.

"That was in the winter," said Zoe.

"I can't wait here until winter," said Polly. "I have to get back to the store."

Hee, hee! That was funny!

MARGARINE
AND MARBLES

The other grownups had things to do too, so Tom, Sanjeev, and the twins were left on their own.

"We can't wait for the road to get icy," said Tom, "but we could find something else to make it slippery. Let's go and ask Mom."

Tom's mom was baking in the kitchen.

21

Squelch!

Pip was playing with a tub of margarine.

"Oh Pip!" said Tom's mom. "Look at the mess — someone could slip!"

"Margarine!" said Tom. "That's what we need!"

"Whatever for?" asked Tom's mom.

"For the crate," said Zoe. "Tom thinks we could move it if we made it more slippery."

"Margarine is certainly slippery," laughed Tom's mom, "but I don't think there's enough here."

"What else is slippery?" asked Tom. "There must be something we can use. Let's go and ask Dad."

Tom's dad was busy in the garage.

"Pass me that can of engine grease please, Tom," he said.

"Oh yuk!" said Chloe. "It's all slimy."

"Is it slippery enough to make the crate slide?" asked Tom.

"It might be," said Dad, "but you can't put messy grease on the road."

"What's in here?" asked Sanjeev, picking up a large tin and shaking it.

"That's Dad's . . ." Tom started to answer, but at that moment the lid came off the tin and hundreds of colored glass marbles poured over the floor.

As Chloe stepped forward to grab the tin, the marbles rolled beneath her feet and she skidded across the garage.

Whoah! Help!

"Are you OK?" asked Tom's dad, as he helped Chloe up from a pile of flower pots.

"I think so," said Chloe.

"That's it!" said Tom. "Dad, can we use them to put under the crate?"

"No, you can't!" said Tom's dad. "That's my prize marble collection. I've had them since I was a boy."

A BETTER IDEA

After they had picked up every marble, the children went indoors to Tom's room.

"Those marbles rolling around made me think of the pyramids in Egypt," said Tom, hunting through a pile of books on the floor.

What are you looking for?

"Here. Look!"

In the book was a picture showing some men from long ago moving a huge stone. They put the stone on top of some round wooden logs. As they pushed the stone the logs rolled and the massive stone slid forward.

"That's just like Chloe sliding on the marbles!" said Zoe.

"I'm not a lump of stone!" said Chloe.

"Won't the stone slip forward too far and come off the logs?" asked Sanjeev.

Tom turned the page. "No," he said. "Look
– as the stone moves forward, the men pick
up the last log and replace it at the front."

The children ran downstairs to show the book to Tom's mom and dad.

"Now that's an idea that might just work," said Tom's dad. "Well done, kids!"

We've got a plan!

"I think I even know where we can get some logs," said Tom's mom. "Polly is putting up a new fence, and she has lots of round fence posts."

Pip got very excited. "We're going to move the monster!" he shouted, jumping up and down.

"Whatever it is, it's not a monster, silly," said Tom.

FENCE POSTS
AND FORKLIFTS

Soon the street was full of willing helpers.

Polly arrived in her van with the fence posts, and Tom explained what they were going to do.

"How will we get the logs under the crate?" asked John the letter carrier.

"We'll have to lift it somehow," said Tom. "Has anyone got any ideas?"

"We have a forklift truck," said Bill from the garage.

"It couldn't lift this enormous crate," said Brenda.

"No," said Bill, "but I think it could lift one end at a time, enough to roll the posts underneath."

While Brenda fetched the forklift truck, Tom's mom handed around slices of freshly baked chocolate cake.

"This is yummy!" said Zoe. "I'm glad the margarine went in the cake and not on the road!"

Yum!

Soon Brenda
returned with the
forklift. By raising
each end of the crate
in turn, they managed to slide several posts
under the crate.

At last they were ready to go.

Everyone got into place behind the crate,
ready to push one last time.

"If this doesn't work, the crate will just
have to stay here," said Tom's mom.

"Mrs. Ramsbottom won't like that!"
laughed the twins.

"It's going to work, I know it is," said Tom.
"Come on, everybody!"

"One, two, three, PUSH!" called Tom's dad.

Everyone pushed as hard as they could.

Nothing happened.

Push!

And again!

"And again!" called
Joe, "One, two, three, PUSH!"
This time, something did
happen. The crate wobbled, the posts
began to roll and, very slowly, the
crate began to slide forward.

"It's working!" shouted Tom.

Tom's dad and Bill placed another post at the front of the crate as it slid forward.

"One, two, three, PUSH!" called Joe.

Once again, the crate slid forward.

Each time they pushed, the crate seemed to move a little faster. Tom's dad and Bill had to be quicker at replacing the posts at the front of the crate.

The crate moved faster, and faster, and . . .

Come back!

Come on, you guys!

CRASH!

Stop that crate!

"Stop!" shouted a voice they hadn't heard before. "Stop, stop it now!"

They turned to see a lady in a green uniform shouting and waving her arms.

"Stop!" she yelled.

But the crate, which had been too heavy to start, was now too heavy to stop.

Stop that crate!

Oh no!

It slid forward off the posts, crashed into a tree, and split open.

Everyone stood staring with their mouths open.

There, standing in the middle of the wreckage, was a very bewildered baby elephant.

Wow!

He's so cute!

The lady in the green uniform came running up. She was from the wildlife park two miles outside the town.

"We've been so worried," she said. "When he didn't arrive this morning we called the police. They told me a large crate had been left in your street."

The elephant wasn't hurt at all. In fact, he seemed to be enjoying all the attention.

"No wonder it was so hard to move!" said Zoe.

"How are you going to get him back to the wildlife park?" asked Tom's dad.

"We'll have to walk," said the keeper. "It's not too far."

Thank goodness you found him!

"At least it'll be easier than all that pushing or pulling!" said Tom.

The children grabbed a bucket of water for the elephant to drink and a large bunch of bananas in case he was hungry.

The keeper thanked them, and gave them free tickets to visit the wildlife park. Then she let Pip ride the elephant to the end of the street.

"What's his name?" asked Pip, as the keeper lifted him down.

"I think I'm going to call him Pip," said the keeper.

Everyone thought that was a wonderful idea, and they all promised to visit Pip the elephant in his new home.

"Goodbye, Pip!" They all waved as Pip and his keeper set off along the road.

"Come on, you guys," said Tom's dad. "We've got some cleaning up to do – and pick up those banana peels before somebody slips!"

Cool bananas!

FORCES

What is a force?

Forces are the push and the pull on an object. For example, if Tom pushes Pip's stroller in this direction:

⬅

then the stroller will go in this direction:

Wheeeee!

If the size of the forces on an object are the same and the direction is opposite, then the forces can balance.

If one force is bigger than the other, then objects will speed up, slow down, or change direction.

Aargh!

FRICTION

The heavier an object, the more force is needed to push or pull it. This is partly because of friction.

Friction is useful because without it there would be no grip! Things would just slip and slide away from each other. When two surfaces rub against each other, like an elephant and pavement, that causes friction.

Friction increases as the pressure between two surfaces increases.

The heavier an object, the greater the pressure.

This makes heavier objects harder to push or pull.

There is more friction, or grip, between rough surfaces than between smooth ones.

If one of the surfaces is smooth, it is easier to push or pull something.

The surface of the ice is smoother than the pavement. That is why Tom can push the elephant now.

BOWLING

Make your own pins!

Here is a fun game you can play, using force!

You will need:

6 large, empty plastic drink bottles

Sand, or water, for weight

A tennis ball

How to make them:

1 Wash the bottles out well.

2 Pour the sand or water in them. Put different amounts in each bottle so that each bottle is a different weight.

3 Screw the lids on tightly.

4 Then line them up outside and roll the tennis ball at them. See if you can knock them all down in one go!

You might have to use more force to knock the heavier ones over.